On the Moon

Anna Milbourne

Illustrated by
Benji Davies

Reading consultant: Alison Kelly
Roehampton University

This story is about a rocket,

astronauts

and the Moon.

The Moon is
very far away.

Astronauts have been there.

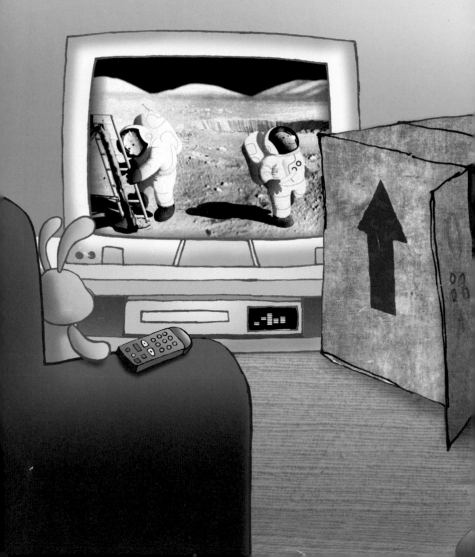

The astronauts sat at
the very top of a rocket.

Five
Four
Three
Two
One...

**LIFT
OFF!**

The rocket flew
into space.

It took four whole days
to reach the Moon.

The astronauts landed
in a little spaceship.

They put on space
suits to go outside.

The Moon was quiet
and very dusty.

There were mountains

and huge holes
called craters.

The astronauts felt
light and floaty.

BOUNCE!

BOUNCE!

They could jump
really far.

16

They explored
in a Moon buggy.

They took photos

and collected rocks.

They even put
up a flag.

They looked at our world. It was very far away!

Then they blasted off
for home.

The buggy, the flag and their footprints are still there.

Would you like to go to the Moon?

PUZZLES

Puzzle 1

Can you find these things in the picture?

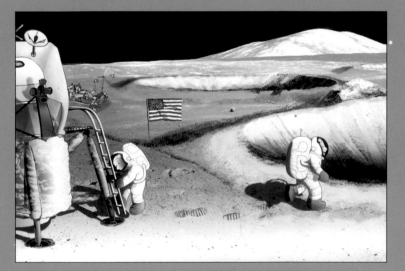

astronauts   Moon buggy

flag   craters

helmets   footprints

Puzzle 2

Can you spot the differences between these two pictures?

There are six to find.

Puzzle 3

Can you pick the right sentence for each picture?

They put on space suits.
They put on silly shoes.

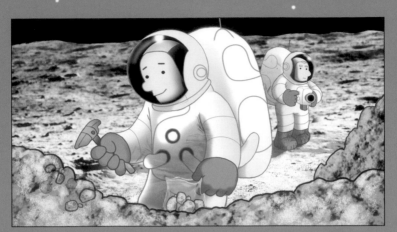

They collected socks.

They collected rocks.

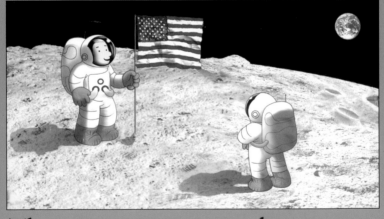

They even put up a bag.

They even put up a flag.

Answers to puzzles

Puzzle 1

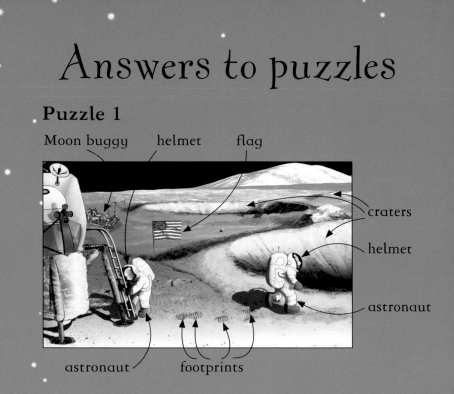

Moon buggy   helmet   flag

craters

helmet

astronaut

astronaut   footprints

Puzzle 2

Puzzle 3

They put on space suits.

They collected rocks.

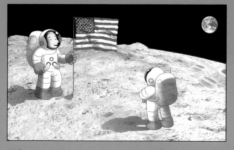

They even put up a flag.

Consultant: Stuart Atkinson
Design: Pete Taylor
Cover design: Non Taylor
Series editor: Lesley Sims

Photographs © NASA; photographs of Earth © Digital Vision

This edition first published in 2011 by Usborne Publishing Ltd.,
Usborne House, 83-85 Saffron Hill, London EC1N 8RT, England.
www.usborne.com Copyright © 2011, 2004 Usborne Publishing Ltd.

USBORNE FIRST READING
Level Two

Stone Soup
USBORNE FIRST READING
Retold by Lesley Sims
Illustrated by Georgien Overwater

The Baobab Tree
USBORNE FIRST READING
Retold by Louie Stowell
Illustrated by Laure Fournier

The Tortoise and the Eagle
USBORNE FIRST READING
Retold by Rob Lloyd Jones
Illustrated by Eugenia Nobati

The Genie in the Bottle
USBORNE FIRST READING
Retold by Rosie Dickins
Illustrated by Sara Rojo

USBORNE FIRST READING
Level One

USBORNE FIRST READING

The **Fox** and the **Crow**

Retold by Mairi Mackinnon
Illustrated by Rocío Martinez

USBORNE FIRST READING

The **Three Wishes**

Retold by Lesley Sims
Illustrated by Elisa Squillace

USBORNE FIRST READING

The **Lion** and the **Mouse**

Retold by Mairi Mackinnon
Illustrated by Frank Endersby

USBORNE FIRST READING

The **Sun** and the **Wind**

Retold by Mairi Mackinnon
Illustrated by Francesca di Chiara